THE HONEY DRUM

THE HONEY DRUM

*seven tales
from Arab lands*

Gwendolyn MacEwen

◤ MOSAIC PRESS

Canadian Cataloguing in Publication Data

MacEwen, Gwendolyn, 1941-
  The honeydrum

ISBN 0-88962-228-0 (bound). - ISBN 0-88962-227-2 (pbk.)

1. Tales - Arab countries.   2. Arabs - Folklore.
I. Title.

PS8525.E95H65 1983   j398.2'0917'4927   C84-098111-2
PZ8.1.M14Ho 1983

Published by Mosaic Press, P.O. Box 1032, Oakville, Ontario L6J 5E9, Canada.

Published with the assistance of the Canada Council and the Ontario Arts Council.

Typeset by Speed River Graphics.
Design by Doug Frank.
Printed and bound in Canada.

ISBN 0-88962-227-2 paper
ISBN 0-88962-228-0 cloth

Distributed in the United States by Flatiron Books, 175 Fifth Avenue, Suite 814, New York, N.Y. 10010, U.S.A.

Distributed in the U.K. by John Calder (Publishers) Ltd., 18 Brewer Street, London, W1R 4AS, England.

Distributed in New Zealand and Australia by Pilgrims South Press, P.O. Box 5101, Dunedin, New Zealand.

CONTENTS

AUTHOR'S NOTE

Of the seven tales in this collection, two - *THE BLACK GOAT* and *THE GHOUL*, are original pieces, while the remaining five are derived from oral and written folk tales and legends as well known in the Arabic-speaking world as *Cinderella* or *Hansel and Gretel* are in the West. *THE SLEEPERS* is taken from the tale of the seven sleepers found in the Koran; it has, like other 'borrowed' stories, undergone some changes in names and details. *FOUR WAYS TO FORTUNE* is closer to a translation of one of the tales from *Kalilah and Dimnah*, a collection of stories in some ways resembling *The Thousand and One Nights*. None of these tales, however, is literally translated from the Arabic, since it has been my purpose to re-create their atmosphere and charm in English in as relaxed a manner as possible.

Gwendolyn MacEwen

THE
HONEY
DRUM

One day all the important men in the great city of Antar met to discuss what sort of gift they might give to their good king Ali, for he had been sad for a long time, thinking that his people had forgotten him. Now it was a very hot day and the elders of the city sat sipping lemonade through long straws and letting servants fan them with great fans of ostrich feathers, and it was a long time before anyone came up with an idea. Finally one old man spoke up. 'Noble sheikhs,' said he, 'I think the greatest gift we could give to our king would be a horse, black as the night, with hooves swift as lightning and eyes bright as stars. What say you to this?'

He sat on his cushion and waited as his companions discussed the idea, but it was not long before the discussion turned into an argument, for none of these noble gentlemen had ever been able to agree upon a single thing. Indeed, they scarcely agreed upon the colour of the sky, so it is not strange that they could not agree upon a black horse with hooves swift as lightning and eyes bright as stars. Presently another sheikh managed to raise his voice higher than the others so that he might be heard.

'My friends!' he shouted, 'We all know that it is impossible to find such an animal as this in the whole kingdom. Would anyone of you care to go into the desert where the wild Beduoin dwell, and journey twelve days and twelve nights to find such a beast?'

And everyone mumbled, 'No, not I, not I . . .'

'Then,' said the sheikh, 'I suggest another gift. I say that every man and woman in the city should donate some gold to make for king Ali a great golden belt as wide as a river and as bright as the sun. What say you to this?'

And he sat on his cushion and once again the arguments began. Now no one at all agreed upon this second idea, and the truth of the matter was that no one wished to give up his gold to make a belt for the king.

'Has not king Ali enough gold as it is?' cried one. And then everyone said, 'Ah, by Allah, he has enough.'

Suddenly a voice was heard which came from the corner of the room, and everyone turned around to see who was speaking. When they saw that it was only young Ahmed the most foolish boy in the entire city, they laughed, for everyone knew that Ahmed didn't know the night from the day, or the front of a donkey from the back.

'And what is *your* suggestion, Foolish One?' they teased him.

'I know exactly what the king would like,' said Ahmed.

'And what is that, Ridiculous One?'

'A honey drum,' said Ahmed.

Now at this suggestion the sheikhs nearly fell onto the floor with laughter, and one of them spilled lemonade all down his beard, and another laughed so hard that he revealed that he had no teeth, a fact which he had been hiding for almost five years.

'And why, in the name of Allah, a honey drum?' they cried.

'Because,' said Ahmed, 'Everyone knows the king likes honey more than anything else in the world. He eats it for breakfast, for dinner, for supper, he eats it in mid-morning, in mid-afternoon, and even at mid-night. I suggest that every citizen donate from his house one cup of honey, and in the end there will be enough honey to fill an enormous drum, enough for king Ali to eat for the rest of his life. And even the poorest family can afford to give one small cup!'

Now the laughter soon faded to silence, for there was wisdom in Ahmed's words, and how much easier it was to part with a mere cup of honey than a piece of gold! After much thinking the sheikhs came at last to an agreement; a honey drum was the ideal gift.

Glad to have solved their problem, the elders all went home and passed the rest of the day drinking tea and coffee and sitting in the shade of their gardens.

Now when the day came for all the people of the city to line up in the main square and pour their cups of honey into the big drum, young Ahmed was very pleased with himself, and the reason he was pleased is a shame to tell, but it must be told. He had decided that he was going to get the better of everyone and save himself the expense of a cup of honey by pouring a cup of water into the drum instead. After all, he told himself, who was going to notice a single cup of water in amongst thousands of cups of honey? So Ahmed took his place in the line, and when his turn came he poured in his cup of water, then he hastily went on his way, smiling to himself all the while.

The next day king Ali came to the square to receive his gift, for the drum was too heavy to be taken to the palace. When he saw the thousands of people crowded in the square, he was filled with joy, for he felt that his people loved him after all.

'I wonder what's inside the drum?' he asked himself, with great excitement he took off the lid and looked inside.

But it was a long time before he lifted his head and looked at the thronging crowds, and when he did, his face was dark with anger and the people drew back, afraid.

'Do you think,' he cried, 'That your king is the thirstiest man in the world? Or that,

perhaps, he needs to take more baths? Is that why you have presented him with a drum full of water, nothing but water?'

And the people, each one of whom had thought to get the better of everyone else in the same way as the foolish Ahmed, ran from the square back to their homes and bolted their doors behind them. And in a very few days the great drum was empty, for the sun and the air evaporated every drop. And there it stands, in the city of Antar, to this very day.

ABDULLAH AND THE WISE OLD MAN

Abdullah was a very ambitious boy who spent his time travelling up and down the land in search of fame and fortune. When he grew a little older he became a travelling merchant and he had a modestly-sized caravan which he led through all the caravan routes in the country - over the hills and mountains and through the burning deserts where jackals howled by night and deadly scorpions bit.

But because Abdullah was ambitious he longed for more, and he often dreamed of himself as the wealthiest man in the land, drinking sherbet and sitting on silk cushions and having private musicians play for him well into the night. He grew tired of being a mere merchant, and it was just at the time when he was most fed up with his life that he chanced upon a strange old man in one of the remote towns on the edge of the desert.

Now the old man's name was Salah, and he possessed many ancient books and ancient secrets, and one day he came to Abdullah bearing a small flask of liquid which, when held up to the sunlight, shone with every colour in the rainbow.

'What do you wish to sell me, Old One?' asked Abdullah. 'A bottle of coloured water?'

Salah laughed and his small black eyes narrowed. 'This is no water, merchant,' he said, 'But the most precious liquid you will ever see in your entire life. I have guarded this flask for twenty years since it was given to me by an old Beduoin who wished to be rid of it forever. You see, a drop of this, painted over your right eyelid, will make you a wealthy man for life!'

Abdullah laughed. 'If it's so precious, why did the last owner wish to be rid of it, O Wise One?'

'Because it is the stuff of Satan,' answered Salah. 'And if it were ever painted over the left eye, the results would be very different indeed. One would go blind in that case.' Then in a warning voice he added, 'In the most beautiful of flowers there is always a thorn.'

Now Abdullah was so tired of his lot that he decided to try some of the liquid, and after paying the old man a large sum of money, he allowed Salah to paint his right eyelid.

'Nothing has happened,' he complained five minutes later.

But Salah smiled and said, 'Go away now, and you will see.'

So Abdullah left the town and made his way back to one of the great cities, and within a very short time he found himself a very rich man indeed. He owned a whole palace and a stable of fine Arabian horses, and dozens of servants and everything a man could possibly wish for. For a year he enjoyed himself as only a king might. But at the end of the year he began to wonder about what Salah had said.

'He was tricking me,' thought Abdullah, 'About the left eye. Surely if I painted the other eye I would be twice as rich as I am now.'

And so he left his palace and made a second journey to the village at the edge of the desert, and when he found Salah he said, 'Wise One, I can pay you a thousand times more than I did before, if only you'll paint my left eyelid with your wonderful fluid.'

'I have warned you about that,' sighed the old man.

'O come come, I know you just wanted more money,' Abdullah said, 'You can't fool me.'

Very sadly Salah brought the flask to Abdullah and painted his left eyelid as he was asked, and Abdullah smiled with satisfaction all the while. But when he turned to leave he found that he couldn't see a thing.

'Help me, Wise One!' he cried, 'I've gone blind!'

'In the most beautiful flower there is always a thorn,' said Salah. 'And he who desires more than he needs will feel the thorn.'

Then Abdullah wandered out into the desert and because he could not find food or water he soon became very weak, and not long after a hungry lion who was prowling around saw him, and ate him for his midday meal.

THE FOX AND THE HYENA

One day a very clever fox was taking a stroll in the countryside, when suddenly he saw something falling from the sky. It looked like a very large animal, and he jumped out of the way to avoid being hit. But when he saw the thing lying on the ground, he went over and examined it, and found that it was not an animal at all, but a fur coat.

'An eagle must have found it,' he thought, 'And tried to eat it, and then dropped it from the sky when he discovered it was nothing but a coat.'

Considering himself very lucky, the fox picked up the coat and wore it to protect himself from the cool winds, and went on his way. Soon he passed the caves of the hyenas, and the strongest hyena saw him and asked:

'Where did you get such a fine coat, fox?'

'Well, I'm a tailor,' said the fox, 'And it's my job to make such garments.'

'Then you must make one for me,' the hyena said.

Now the fox saw a very good way to get himself some free food, so he said, 'Alright, I'll do it. But you must bring me seven sheep, for I need the skins.'

The hyena agreed, and the next day the fox found himself with seven delicious fat sheep to eat for the next month. And after he ate each one he threw the skins away, for of course he had no idea how to make a coat. And every day the hyena came and asked him, 'Is my coat ready yet?'

And the fox would answer, 'I'm still doing the sleeves'. And then he said, 'I'm still doing the buttonholes.' And when the hyena started to get very impatient and angry that he had not finished, the fox said, 'Look, I need three more sheep to have enough skin for the collar.'

So the hyena brought him three more sheep, but now he was suspicious of the fox, and he watched him secretly as he ate, and saw him throw the skins away. Now the anger of a hyena is a terrible thing, and this hyena was terribly angry and he swore he would kill the fox for cheating him. The fox began to run away but the hyena grabbed him by the tail and pulled and pulled until the tail came right off. The fox ran away without a tail and he heard the hyena laugh and shout:

'I'll get you yet, you thief! You're the only fox in the land without a tail, and I'll recognize you anywhere, so take care!'

Now although the fox was safe for the moment, he was very worried about what might happen to him in the future if he ever met up with the hyena again. But being a clever fox, he thought of a plan to save himself. He gathered together all his fellow foxes and told them that he knew of a vineyard closeby where they could eat fat ripe grapes all night without being caught. But every fox, he said, had to bring a rope to have himself tied to his own grapevine, so that he wouldn't be tempted to eat from the vines of another fox if the grapes there were fatter.

The foxes thought that this was a fair plan, and the same night they all went to the vineyard where the grapes glowed purple in the moonlight. The clever fox led them into the vineyard and tied each of their tails to a vine, and left them alone to eat to their hearts' delight. Then, after an hour had passed, the clever fox went to the top of the hill nearby and cried,

'Run! Run for your lives! The farmer is coming!'

And all the foxes tried to run away, but

their tails were tied, so they pulled harder and harder until at last they were free. And they ran away from the vineyard leaving their tails behind them.

Now the clever fox was safe, for the hyena would never know which one of the foxes he was.

THE
BLACK
GOAT

E veryone used to say that Sayed was the strangest boy in the mountain village of Tel Ahmar. In fact some even whispered that he was the strangest boy in the whole land. Now it wasn't only because his eyes were the blackest eyes anyone had seen, or because his hair was the blackest hair, or even because he had a black goat as a pet. No, it wasn't because of any of these things that people spoke of him in whispers. But he had an odd way of doing things and an even odder way of speaking which made the villagers wonder about him. For instance, he always played alone, and whether this was because he didn't like the other boys or the other boys didn't like him, no one seemed to know. And when he spoke he spoke with a voice soft as a stream that flows underground, and when you looked into his eyes it was like looking

into two deep forbidden wells in the desert. And he always laughed at the wrong time, or didn't laugh at the right time, and when he smiled it was as though he knew something that you didn't know.

People started to say that Sayed had a secret, a deep and terrible secret and that was why he acted so strangely.

'Where did he come from?' asked the men.

'No one knows,' answered the women.

And it was true that no one knew, for one day many years ago when Sayed was only nine years old, he had wandered into the village with his pet black goat, and though the village elders questioned him for hours about his home and his parents, he had never told them anything. A kind family had adopted him and treated him as their own son, but even they never learned from where he came, for when they asked, he only answered, 'From beyond the Hill of the Lion and beyond the Hill of the Ram; don't ask me who I am!' And that was not much for them to go on.

Even his name was not his own, but one given to him by his foster parents.

And no one had any idea where the Hill of the Lion or the Hill of the Ram was.

So Sayed grew up in the village of Tel Ahmar, and when he reached the age of thirteen he got into the very strange habit of wandering off every evening into the surrounding hills, and since he never got home before midnight, his foster parents began to worry about him very much indeed.

'Sayed, where is it you go every night?' pleaded his foster mother.

'Over the mountain's ridge, and under the secret bridge, beyond the Hill of the Sheep, to where two rivers meet,' he said.

Now this did not do any good, for the mother had never heard of any of those places, although she had lived all her life in that part of the land.

'Why does your goat go with you?' asked the father.

'He leads the way,' answered Sayed.

Now one night the parents grew so worried that the father decided that the next time Sayed went out he would follow him. And the very next evening when darkness fell and Sayed slipped out of the gates of the courtyard with his goat, the father put on a heavy robe and went out after him, keeping always a little distance behind to avoid being seen. They went down the mountainside, and at the bottom there was a river with a bridge, which the father had never seen before, and beyond the bridge, another hill which he had never seen either, shaped like a sheep, and beyond that, a place where two rivers met.

And there was a great rock, and the goat walked three times around it, and on the third turn the father gasped with unbelief, for the goat was no longer a goat but a young man the same age as Sayed. The father leaned forward and tried to hear what the

two were saying. And what he heard was
very strange indeed.

'We have been too long among the
people of the world.' said the goat who had
become a boy. 'It is time for us to return to
our land forever.'

And the father saw Sayed become very
sad, and he hung his head before answering
his friend.

'I've grown to like the people so much,'
he said, 'It's hard to leave, it's very hard. . .'

But the goat who had become a boy said,
'Have you forgotten the pledge you made?

Each of us must spend five years on earth and five years only; then we must return to our land. It is the command of our fathers, and the five years are up tonight.'

And then Sayed and his friend circled once again around the great rock, and vanished.

The father returned home very late that night and his face was pale, and his hands trembled as though he had seen a spirit.

'What is it?' asked his wife. 'What have you seen?'

'Strange things,' said the father, 'Stranger than I can tell.'

'And where is Sayed?' she asked.

'Beyond the Hill of the Lion and beyond the Hill of the Ram,' the father said.

And the kind couple did not sleep for many nights, for they thought that Sayed might return, but he never did.

THE
GHOUL

In the desert there lives a very horrible creature which the Arabs call the Ghoul. Now it would not be so bad if the Ghoul had only one ugly shape, but the problem is she has many shapes, and she changes from one to the other as she likes. And as well as having hundreds of shapes, she has thousands of different voices and she uses whichever one suits her at any time. In a moment you will see why those voices are so useful to her.

There was once a young boy called Saud who was always busy amusing himself in a hundred ways; he liked to pull lizards out from under the rocks by their tails; he had a special box for catching birds which he used to check each morning; but most important of all, he had a pet hawk which his father had given him on his thirteenth birthday. Now his father was the sheikh, the head of the

tribe, and he told Saud that in a few years, after the hawk was trained, he could join the men of the tribe in a gazelle hunt, when they used the best hawks and the cleverest greyhounds to catch the swiftest gazelles.

But Saud was an impatient boy, and for him a few years was a long time to wait, so one day he decided to steal away from his father's tent just before dawn, taking his pet with him, and go into the desert where he was sure he would catch something — if only a rabbit or a little bird.

The sun rose higher and higher and by the middle of the morning the sand under his feet had begun to burn as hot as his mother's cooking pots, but still he did not see anything. Now it would soon be noon, and they were far from camp, and Saud knew that he must return home to the shelter of the tents, for in the hottest part of the day no Arab dared remain in the desert without protection.

But Saud couldn't understand why he had seen no sign of life all morning; it was very strange indeed that the desert should be so empty - so he walked on a little farther.

Then he heard a voice behind him, a very soft and sweet voice saying, 'Saud my brother, come with me!'

He turned around suddenly and he couldn't believe his eyes, for there, not six feet away from him was his little sister Layla who was only ten years old. He thought she must have followed him from home, yet she did not look tired or hot or thirsty, but as fresh as a flower. She pointed towards the west, and told him that there was a well of cool sweet water not far away, and if he followed her she would lead him to it.

Now Saud was so thirsty and tired that all he could think of was the water, and he didn't bother to ask her how it was that she had walked so far without being as tired as he. She took his hand and led him deeper into the desert.

The sun was so bright and hot by this time that Saud could scarcely see. He felt sorry for his pet hawk, and set it loose to fly higher and higher into the sky and disappear among the clouds.

Then suddenly Saud was so tired that he could walk no more, and he fell down onto the burning sands and went to sleep. And that was the last thing he remembered.

When he awoke he was surprised to find that he was once again in his father's tent. The smell of burnt coffee filled his nostrils, and he heard the sounds of children playing outside. His father the sheikh was leaning over him.

Where am I?' he asked. 'How did I get here? Where's Layla my sister?'

And his father answered, 'When the hawk flew back to the tents this day he made a great noise as though he wanted to tell us something. I gathered together the men of the tribe and we mounted our swiftest camels and rode out into the desert. The hawk led us west, in a straight line, and then he descended, and we found you lying in the sands asleep. Saud, how did you get there? Do you know where you were?'

Saud shook his head.

'Well you were only a few feet away from the Pool of the Shifting Sands. If you had walked only one or two minutes more, you would have fallen into it and sunk to the very bottom. How did you get there?'

'But she led me there!' Saud cried.

'Who?' asked the father, his face growing pale. 'Who led you there?'

'Why, little Layla of course, ' Saud said. 'Didn't you find her there with me? She said she knew where there was a well, and she was taking me to it.'

Then the face of the sheikh became

even paler, and his voice shook as he spoke.

'Your little sister Layla was with us all day, here in the tents. Whoever led you into the most dangerous part of the desert was not she, but someone who took her shape and her voice. . .'

Saud shivered, for he knew the answer now, even before his father told him.

'By Allah, my son, you have seen the Ghoul!'

THE
SLEEPERS

Once a very long time ago, there were seven good men who lived in a very wicked city whose people worshipped statues and images as gods. The seven good men worshipped only one god - Allah the Mighty and Merciful, but they had to worship him in secret, for the king did not like to hear about Allah. He preferred to have a good time drinking wine and listening to stories all through the night, and his city was very wealthy from the sale of charms and statues of the false gods.

Now one day the king heard that a group of these holy men were going between the people in the streets and markets and telling them of the wonders and miracles of Allah. He became very angry at this, and a little afraid, also, for he secretly feared that perhaps the One God was indeed mightier than he. So he called together the guards of the palace and his finest horsemen and commanded them to go and drive the holy men out of the city.

But one of the guards dared to disagree with him and he spoke up.

'Your Highness— what if this Allah is as mighty as they say, what if he makes a miracle, or takes revenge upon us?'

'Fool!' cried the king, 'Do you want me to pull out all your teeth and leave one for the sake of toothache! Go!'

So the king's horsemen went and drove the holy men out of the city. They fled to the hills where there were caves which might hide them while they rested, and one by one they entered a large cave, lay down, and fell into a deep sleep, so tired were they from their running.

But this was no ordinary sleep; it is strange to tell, but it must be told; it was a sleep which lasted *three hundred years*. Great Allah looked with favour upon these good and humble men and made for them a miracle which all the world might one day know. And the cave where they slept was safe from anyone who might pass by, for the sun's rays never once in three hundred years touched its entrance, and a man passing would never know it was there.

Now when the holy men awoke, it was another age and another time. And the land had passed through many wars, and kings had come and gone, and many things had changed. But they had no way of knowing how long they had slept — to them it had been like a single night. They felt hungry, very hungry indeed, and they decided that one of them should go into the city alone and bring back food.

Now this was a dangerous idea, for if one of them should be recognized they would all be in serious trouble once more, but they decided it was wiser to risk the chance of being discovered than to die from hunger. So one of them set out for the city, but when he arrived at its gates he was filled with a strange wonder. Where were the rug salesmen that used to sell their wares at the gates? Where was the old woman who sold the best cabbages and tomatoes in the city? He could see none of these familiar figures in their usual place, and he was very confused indeed.

But his confusion was to grow even greater, for when he went inside the city to the marketplace, he saw that many of the shops had changed their signs and their wares, and the people were using expressions when they spoke which he had never heard before. He tried to forget his confusion, and picked up a few loaves of bread and some cheese, and took them to the store-owner.

Then he gave the man enough money to pay for them, and started to walk away.

'Hey, you there!' called the store-owner. 'Come back here!'

He turned around, wondering who was calling him.

'You there, I want to see you!' the man cried again.

He returned to the shop and asked him what was wrong. The shopkeeper held out the money he had given him and asked, 'What's this?'

'What's what?' he asked, more confused than ever.

'This money! What kind of money is this supposed to be!' and he held out his hand to show him the coins.

'Why . . . it's money of course,' replied the holy man. 'Is there something wrong with it?'

'*Wrong!*' cried the shopkeeper. I've never seen money like this in my life . . . why it looks hundreds of years old, for one thing. Look — the name of the king written on the coins — that's not our king, that's king Aziz, and he ruled three hundred years ago! What sort of joke are you playing on me, fellow?'

Now the holy man became very nervous, and he began to sense that something very unusual and strange had happened to him and his companions. His only thought was to get out of this city immediately and return to the cave. He ran out into the streets, and without looking in either direction, made a straight course to the city gates. From there he continued running towards the hills.

But he was not running alone, for the shopkeeper had been suspicious enough to send out a few men on horseback to follow him a little ways behind and see where he was going. When they saw him disappear into the cave in the hills, they did not pursue him any farther, but went back to the city and reported the news to the king.

The new king who ruled the city was as cruel and suspicious as king Aziz had been,

and he had heard many stories from the wise
man in the palace about the group of holy
men who were sent out of the city three
hundred years ago. Now he consulted his
most famous wise man and asked him what
he thought about the man who fled to the
cave.

The wise man answered with a trembling voice that he believed this man who
appeared suddenly in the market place with
his old-fashioned clothes and old money . . .
might be none other than one of the famous
holy men who king Aziz had driven away.

'And why do you believe such nonsense!' cried the king.

'My lord, there have been many signs in the skies . . .' whispered the wise man.

The next day the king himself went out to the hills and took with him many of his guards. They dismounted, and climbed up the walls of one of the stony hills until they spotted the entrance to the cave, and the king sent two of his guards inside while the rest waited.

A few minutes later they reappeared, their faces white and their hands trembling with shock.

'What is it, what is it?' cried the king. 'What have you seen?'

And one of them fell to the king's feet and cried, 'My lord, we entered the cave and saw seven men sitting inside; they were dressed in white like holy men of old, and they were talking together in quiet voices. When they saw us, one of them got up to approach us, but at that very moment, Your Majesty, — *every one of them* fell down and died!'

Now the king could not believe such a

story and he himself went inside the cave to see what was within. But his own eyes told him the truth, and when he stepped outside again his face was as pale as the others.

'This is some sort of miracle,' he said. 'I don't like it, and I can't understand it, but some god has done it, and we must respect it.'

Then they returned to the palace and he spoke once again to his wise men and asked them what he should do about the cave. The wise man suggested that he build a temple beside it, a temple to Allah, the god of the seven men. But the king did not agree; it was his idea finally to seal up the cave forever and forget the matter completely. So the cave was sealed and no man ever entered it again.

It is said that a temple was discovered on the same spot many hundreds of years later, long after all the kings and all the people had accepted Allah as their god. But no one can be sure of this, unless he journeys there and sees for himself.

FOUR WAYS
TO
FORTUNE

Once there were four companions — the first was the son of a king and the second was the son of a nobleman and the third was the son of a merchant and the fourth was the son of a common labourer. They journeyed together and wandered together, owning nothing except the clothes on their backs. They met many hardships and began to grow weary, and the king's son said:

'Well, whatever will be will be, and all we can do is wait and see what happens to us. We can't change the future, for only Allah knows it.'

Then the merchant's son spoke up. 'I don't agree with that!' he said. 'The best thing in life is Intelligence, and if one is Intelligent he can gain whatever he needs.'

Then the nobleman's son argued, 'You're both wrong! The best thing in life is

Beauty, for Beauty gives us everything.'

Finally the labour's son gave his own opinion. 'Industry and Hard Work are better than all of these, and that's that!' he said.

They walked on until they reached the town of Matrun. They found a place to sleep for the night, and in the morning when they awoke, three of them said to the labourer's son: 'Go out and earn for us some food for the day, by that Hard Work which you believe in.'

So the labourer's son went into the town and asked the first man he saw what kind of work he could do which would earn enough money to feed four people. The man told him that there was nothing better than cutting wood, so he cut wood all the day, and

66

for his labours he earned half a silver coin.
He bought with it what he could, and before
returning to his companions, he wrote on
the gates of the town:

*One day's Hard Work earned half a
silver coin.*

That night the four companions ate a
simple meal, and when they awoke next
morning they said to the nobleman's son:
'Go into the town and by the Beauty which
you believe in, earn enough to feed us.'

So the nobleman's son started out, thinking to himself, 'What will I do? I'm ashamed to return without anything!' And when he reached the town he leaned against a tree, hoping that an idea would come to him. As he was resting there, an artist happened to pass by and see him. He marvelled at the handsomeness of this young man, and so he sent his servants to fetch him and bring him to his house. There he offered him cool water to refresh himself, and then he drew a beautiful picture of him.

Now when the artist displayed the

picture to the people of the town, a rich man saw it and bought it for a good price, so that evening the artist gave the nobleman's son five hundred *dinars* for his trouble. He set out to return to his companions, and as he passed the gates of the town he wrote:

In one day Beauty earned five hundred dinars!

The next morning when the companions woke up they said to the merchant's son: 'Go out into the town and earn something with that Intelligence you believe in.'

So the merchant's son went out; he walked on and on and didn't stop until he was within sight of a ship which was anchored in the harbour not far from the city. Many people had come down to the beach to buy the goods that the ship carried, but when they learned how high the prices were, they said to each other, 'We will never be able to afford to buy anything from that ship unless they lower the prices and make it cheaper for us. Come on, let's go!' And so the people went home, leaving the merchant's son alone.

Now he had a good idea, and he went out to the ship and made a deal with the captain to buy the whole cargo at once for five thousand *dinars*, to be paid later. When the news of the deal reached the merchants of the city, they ran out to see him and began to buy the cargo from him until all of it was sold. Then the merchant's son took the money he had earned and, after paying the money he owed to the ship's captain, he was left with a profit of five thousand silver coins.

Before he returned to his companions he wrote on the gates of the city:

In one day Intelligence earned five thousand silver coins!"

That night the companions ate and drank abundantly, and when they woke on the fourth day they said to the king's son: 'Go out and earn something for us. If it's true that whatever will be will be, then Allah will be generous with you!'

So the king's son set out, and when he reached the gates of the city he sat down near a shop to rest. The news reached him that the king of the city had died in the night, leaving no son or brother to take his place, and as he sat by the gates the funeral procession passed by him. He didn't move from his place, or grieve at the king's death, and when one of the king's guards saw him he cried, 'Who do you think you are, sitting at the gates today of all days? Why aren't you at home, grieving over the death of the king?'

And the guard drove him away from the place, but he returned soon after to watch them burying the king. When the guard saw him a second time he cried, 'By Allah, since you won't move on, I'll put you in prison!' So the king's son was locked up for the night in the dungeon of the palace.

Now the next day the important men of the city held a big meeting to decide who would be their next king. The palace guard arose and said, 'Yesterday I saw a young man sitting at the gates when we were burying the king; he didn't move, or show any sign of grief, and I imprisoned him, for it was bad luck to have him watching us while we worked.'

Then they brought the boy before them and asked him, 'Who are you, stranger, and why did you act as you did?'

And he answered, "I am the son of king Karuned, and when he died, my younger brother gained the kingdom over me. I ran away from my country until I reached your land, and that is why I am here.'

Now when the noblemen heard this they couldn't believe his words, but it happened that one of them had come from the country of king Karuned, and he recognized the boy and fell at his feet. When they saw this, they changed their minds, and decided to make him their king.

As was the custom, they took the new king and paraded him around the city for the people to see him, and when they passed by the city gates, the king saw what his companions had written. He ordered a servant to write beneath their words:

Hard Work and Intelligence and Beauty won't bring man goodness, or save him from evil, if he tries to escape the will of Allah.

When the new king returned to the palace he sat on his bed and asked a servant to go out and summon his companions to him. When they came he gave them much money, enough for them to be rich for the rest of their lives. 'But be sure, my friends,' he told them. 'That it is Allah who provided this for us, and I was rewarded in my life, not by Beauty or Intelligence or Hard Work but by the wisdom of Allah.'

Then he went on to say, 'When I was treated badly by my brother and driven away from my land, I reached this land and I met you, my friends, and I learned that there were people in the world who were as good or even better than me. Now as I sit here in the palace surrounded by my good fortune, I remember the hard times we had together, and I remember that we were happy, even in the midst of our hardships.'

Then an old sheikh who was sitting with them in the room arose and said, 'O King, you have spoken wise words, for you have made us remember that all things in the world, great or small, from the lowest to the highest, are living together under the will of Allah. The generosity and the wisdom of Allah are the same for all men, and we must praise Him.'

And another sheikh arose and spoke after him. 'O King,' he said, 'When I was a small boy I was also a stranger in this land, and I worked as a simple servant and I earned only two *dinars* as my wage. I wanted to give one *dinar* to Allah and keep one for myself and buy what I needed with it, so I went to the market to shop. I saw a man with two pigeons in a cage, and he wanted two *dinars* for them. I didn't want to buy only one pigeon, because I thought they maybe were brothers or man and wife, and if they were separated one of them might die . . . so I bought them both. I took them out of the market and I opened the cage and set them free again, and they alit on a tree nearby. Then I heard them speaking to me:

'O kind man,' they said, 'We thank you for giving us our freedom, and to show our thanks we want to tell you that beneath this very tree there is a buried treasure. Dig and you will find it!'

'Now I didn't believe them at first, but I

approached the tree and dug up a little bit of earth, and Lo! — my spade hit the edge of a wooden box, and when I opened it, I found enough treasure to last me many years. The two pigeons started to fly away then, but I called out to them.

'O birds! You fly between heaven and earth, and you can see what is beneath the very ground! How then, with such talents, could you have been caught in the first place?'

And one of them called back to me:

'Don't you know, O Wise Man, that whatever must be will be and whatever will happen must happen, and no one can change it?'

When the sheikh finished his tale there was a great silence in the room, for each one

in his heart was silently thanking Allah for
his good fortune.

Gwendolyn MacEwen